UXMAL
ALAN
CRANE

NICK AND NAN IN YUCATAN

ALAN CRANE

THOMAS NELSON & SONS

EDINBURGH   NEW YORK   TORONTO

By the Same Author

GLOUCESTER JOE
PEPITA BONITA

Original lithographs drawn on stone by Alan Crane
Printed by George C. Miller in the United States of America

COPYRIGHT 1945 BY ALAN CRANE

This complete edition is produced in
full compliance with the Government's
regulations for conserving paper and
other essential materials

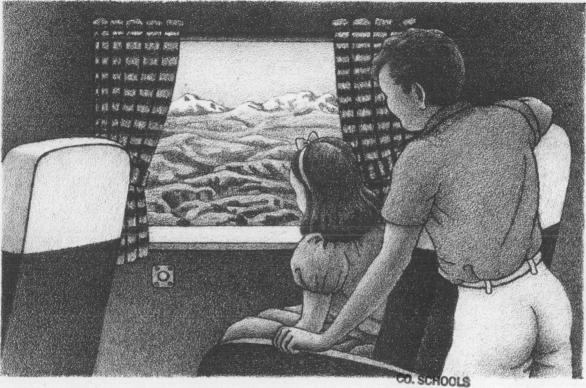

The ground dropped beneath them!

Mother and Father still stood side by side, waving good-by. Soon they became smaller, until at last they were just two little dots at the Mexican airport.

The plane rose higher and higher. Mexico City seemed like a toy town. Nan looked at Nick. Nick looked at Nan. They were off to Yucatan!

"Oh, I wish Mother and Father had come with us," said Nan, and Nick saw that her eyes were brimming with tears.

"So do I," he answered. "And I know they're thinking the same thing. They'd lots rather be here in this plane with us, right now. And they'd like to visit Uncle Fred, too. But business must come first, Father said."

"What if Uncle Fred doesn't meet us?" Nan asked anxiously. "What if we don't know him when we see him? What if he doesn't like us, Nick? And what if we don't like him?"

Nick began to laugh. "There you go again! Sure we've never seen Uncle Fred. How could we, when he's been in Yucatan ever since we were babies? But he's our uncle, just the same. And you know he said in his letter that he's been counting the

days till we get there. Of course we're going to like him. And of course he's going to like us. What's there to worry about, for goodness sake?"

Nan wiped her eyes. "Well," she said, with a watery little smile, "we may be the kind of twins that everybody says look as much alike as two peas in a pod, but we're not a bit the same inside."

Nan was right. The minute people looked at them, they knew they were twins. Nick had light hair, exactly like Nan's. His eyes were the same shade of blue as hers. They were the same height. Even their noses turned up the same way. But inside they were as different as could be. Their mother often called them Hurry and Worry, for Nick was forever bustling about, busy as could be, with plenty of questions about everything. Usually Nan took more time doing things, and she was always worrying about whether they would turn out right.

Nan soon forgot her worries about the uncle she had never met. This was the twins' first airplane ride, and she didn't want to miss a bit of it.

"Look!" exclaimed Nick excitedly. "The mountains aren't high any more— except those two with snow on top."

Nan turned in the direction Nick was pointing. The steward of the huge passenger plane, who had come up beside them, told them that the Indians called the tall peaks "The Smoking Mountain" and "The Sleeping Woman."

It was all so exciting! After they had crossed the mountains, they went over miles of green jungle, far below. Now and then they looked down on a river that was a silver thread in the sun. When at last the jungle disappeared, there was the endless bright blue sea spread out beneath them.

"It's the Gulf of Mexico," explained the steward. "It won't be long now before we'll be landing in Yucatan."

"Father says Yucatan is as flat as a pancake," Nan said, in a worried voice. "What will happen to us if it's all a desert and the water wells dry up?"

The steward grinned. "Just you wait and see!" he said. "Better get your things together, kids. There's Merida now."

Merida! Nan caught her breath. That was where Uncle Fred lived, where he was waiting for them this very minute. That is, she hoped he was waiting for them!

Nick's nose was pressed flat against the window. "I didn't know Merida was as big as that, Nan," he cried.

"Of course it's big," she replied. "It's the capital of Yucatan, isn't it?"

"But where's the Gulf of Mexico gone?" asked Nick, as the plane pointed downward. "I can't see it any more."

"You don't see it because it's twenty-five miles away," the steward told him. "It's over there, at Progresso. Progresso's the place where the big steamers come in to exchange supplies." And he pointed toward the distant horizon.

But Nick and Nan had eyes only for the large city just below. It came nearer and nearer as the plane circled around, getting ready to land. Soon they were bumping along the ground. Then the plane slowed down and stopped.

"Merida!" called the steward. "All out for Merida!"

Nick and Nan were among the first passengers out the door. A big crowd was waiting to meet friends. The twins stood stock still, an anxious little look in Nick's eyes, as well as in Nan's.

Suddenly a deep voice said, "There you are, Nick and Nan! Welcome to Yucatan!"

The twins looked around, and knew at once just which man in the crowd had spoken. He was coming quickly toward them, with the same kind of quiet smile as Father's, and the same shining eyes—their Uncle Fred!

"Father has a lot more hair, though," thought Nan.

Soon they were seated in Uncle Fred's car, on their way to his home in Merida. Now that they had been safely met, Nick bubbled with questions.

"Will we see any Mayans, Uncle Fred? Where do they live? Is it near here? Can we go to see them?"

"Help!" laughed Uncle Fred. "Where did you find out about the Mayans?"

"From a book Father got for us," Nan explained.

"And he told us a lot about them, too," added Nick. "They lived down here even before our Indians came to the United States, I guess."

Before Uncle Fred had time to answer any of Nick's questions, Nan had one.

"Are the Mayans dangerous?" she asked.

Uncle Fred laughed again. "Not any more dangerous than you are," he replied. "In fact, I'm sure you are going to like them very much, especially Fito who is coming to see you tomorrow. Fito's grandmother was a Mayan, a direct descendant of the Mayans of olden times."

"Does Fito live in Merida?" asked Nick. "How old is he? Can he tell us about the ruins?"

"He is just about your age," Uncle Fred told them, "and a fine boy. His father works for me, finding zapote trees in the jungle. Zapote trees are the ones from which we get the chicle that goes into chewing gum. Fito has seen more of the ruins than most of the people who live around here. There are all kinds of Mayan ruins in the jungle, and Fito often goes there with his father."

"Are some of those ruined palaces really two thousand years old?" Nick asked.

"Yes, all of that," said Uncle Fred. "Well, here we are, twins. Here's your home in Yucatan."

The car stopped in front of a pale pink house. Its walls rose right up from the sidewalk just like all the other houses on the street. The tall windows were covered with iron gratings and the great wooden doors were slowly opening.

"Well, well," said Uncle Fred, "if here isn't our Senora Alvarez waiting for us."

In the doorway of the patio stood the old Senora who kept house for Uncle Fred. The wide full skirt of her white dress was trimmed with embroidery as gay and bright as the flowers. The underskirt hung a few inches below, as was the style, and she wore a pink bow in the back of her hair.

"Welcome," she said to Nick and Nan in English, smiling at them. "Welcome very much." And she held out her hands to them.

Nothing could have made the twins feel more at home than having Senora Alvarez speak to them in English. With happy smiles they followed her through a short passageway to a tall iron gate which opened into the patio. Just as in the house that the twins' mother and father rented in Mexico City, Uncle Fred's pink home was built around a lovely little garden, with a bubbling fountain, green plants and bright flowers right inside the four walls. The living room, dining room and kitchen opened off the patio, and from the living room a stairway of tiles led to the bedrooms above.

The twins followed Uncle Fred up the stairway. "Here you are," he said. "This is your bedroom."

Nick and Nan looked about them. It was a very pretty room, with flowers on the tables, and comfortable leather furniture made of calfskin stretched over wooden frames. The balcony looked down on the patio.

But there wasn't a sign of a bed anywhere! Again the worried look came into Nan's eyes. She was very sure she wouldn't enjoy sleeping on the floor!

"Where do we sleep?" Nick asked abruptly.

Uncle Fred laughed and pointed to some large iron hooks in the wall. "Your beds will swing from those," he said. "In Yucatan almost everyone sleeps in hammocks made of hemp. They are much cooler than beds, you know, and it does get pretty hot here. You'll find that our hammocks are mighty comfortable, too. That is, they are if you lie crosswise in them, and at an angle. I'll show you just how to do it this evening."

"That will be fun," the twins agreed. "But why can't we practice right now, Uncle Fred?"

"Because something else is more important right now," replied their uncle. "The Senora has something special waiting for us down in the patio."

A delicious supper was spread on a small table set in the patio garden. There were tamales made of meat, wrapped in banana leaves, tall glasses of cold milk, and for dessert, plenty of guava jelly with crackers.

Nan declared that while she was in Yucatan she was going to learn how to make tamales, and surprise Mother and Father with them. Nick put in a request that she try her hand at guava jelly as well.

"You'll show her how to make it, won't you, Senora?" he asked.

Senora Alvarez nodded and smiled happily. Then she pointed to a tree in the corner of the patio. "From your own guava tree, Mees Nan," she said.

Next morning, when Nan woke up, she didn't open her eyes for a moment. Instead she stretched comfortably and made her hammock swing back and forth. Uncle Fred was right. A hammock was very nice for sleeping.

When she did look around the room, which was full of lovely sunshine, she saw that her twin's hammock was quite empty.

"Nick!" she called anxiously.

"Here I am," he said. "Out on the balcony. Come see all these windmills!"

Nan slid out of her hammock, shoved her feet into her slippers, and ran outside. Nick was already dressed, and looking across Merida's rooftops. In every direction windmills were whirring in the early morning breeze. Housetops and windmills— Merida was full of them.

"I wonder why there are so many?" cried Nan. "Windmills, I mean."

A chuckle from below answered her. Nick and Nan looked down to see Uncle Fred watching them.

"Because we need water, that's why," he told them. "You see, our Yucatan country is a flat crust of limestone and the only water is in underground streams. So if we are going to have water for ourselves, we must bring it up out of the ground. The windmills do that for us. And since we need lots of water, we have lots of windmills. A good many people call Merida 'The City of Windmills.'"

"I like them," declared Nan.

"So do I," said Nick.

"Right now, I like the idea of a little breakfast," said Uncle Fred. "How about it, twins? Hurry along down. Besides, someone is waiting for you."

Nan took a shower in the modern bathroom, and hustled into her clothes. Then she and Nick ran down the stairs together. A dark-skinned boy with a broad smile was standing in the patio with Uncle Fred. It was Fito.

"I am very glad to see you," he said in perfect English. "I hope that you will like Merida."

"We do already," Nan told him.

"It's wonderful," said Nick. And they shook hands with their new friend.

"I thought everyone here would talk in Spanish," Nan said.

"Most of my people do," replied Fito. "But you see for a long time I used to help an American lady who lived here. I would go to the market for her and do many things around her house. She taught me much English, which I taught to my father, too. She always said I would some day visit her in the United States, and perhaps stay there to go to one of the fine big American schools."

Fito paused a moment, then said soberly, "Now I think, though, that I can never do that." With the smile gone from his face, Fito looked so sad that Nan couldn't think of a thing to say.

"Don't worry, Fito," Nick declared. "You can visit us, now. As soon as Father has finished his business in Mexico, we are going home to the United States."

At Nick's words, a faint little smile came back to Fito's lips. But his eyes were still solemn.

"Thank you," he said. "Thank you very much. But I think it cannot be."

Just then the Senora called them to breakfast. Afterwards the twins, with Fito as guide, started downtown to see the big plaza.

Fito first led them along a street that was lined with neat little houses, each of which was a lovely color. Some were soft green. Others were yellow. Still others were pink and lavender.

"How pretty!" exclaimed Nan. "But why aren't any of them white, Fito?"

"Well, you see," replied Fito, "we have a law here that says the houses cannot be painted white or black. The law also says that everyone must put a fresh coat of paint on his house every two years, at least. So the people who own the houses make them the colors they like best. And if they change their minds about what they like, they change the color!"

"Everyone wears white clothes, though," said Nick.

"White clothes are cool," explained Fito. "That is quite important when it is so very hot."

"Are they cooler when they are clean?" Nick asked next. "I've never seen folks so spick-and-span."

Fito smiled proudly. "Maybe you have heard that Merida is one of the cleanest cities in Mexico. We like that. And we try to keep ourselves as clean as our city. Even our poor people have two suits of clothes, at least, so that they can wear a fresh one every day."

When they reached the big plaza they stood under tall, wide-spreading Indian laurel trees. Bright flowers grew here and there, and on all sides they could see the busy life of Merida. The twins were interested in the many horse-drawn carriages, all alike, that were passing around the plaza.

"Coches," Fito said they were called, pronouncing it *ko-chays*. "It means *coaches* in English. They are the taxicabs of Merida."

Shops and even little restaurants, with tables under the arcades on the sidewalk, surrounded the square. An auto dashed by now and then, but there were not very many of them. People in white strolled about, or sat on benches in the square. Shoeshine boys were busy. Many of the women wore costumes just like the Senora Alvarez. Some carried babies on their hips, "like a bundle of sugar," Nan said.

Beyond the old cathedral which faced the square, its two towers reaching to the sky, they came to a small sidewalk restaurant that had especially gay covers on its four tables.

"Shall we not sit down and have a drink of cool cocoanut milk?" asked Fito.

The twins thought the drink delicious. Soon they were quite ready for more exploring, but in an hour they were not sorry to turn homeward. When they came to another plaza, much smaller than the main one by the old cathedral, they welcomed Fito's suggestion that they sit down for a while on the odd little stone benches there.

"I like this," said Nick, settling himself comfortably. Then he turned to Fito. "Why did you say you could never come to visit us?"

"Doesn't your mother want you to leave Yucatan?" asked Nan.

"It isn't that," Fito replied. "Mother wants very much for me to go. Quite a while ago I was all ready to start. And the money for my trip was planned for, too. But something happened."

Fito paused, and again the sad look came into his eyes.

"It was because of the chain that I could not go," he went on after a moment. "You see, when my grandmother grew very old, she gave my mother a chain. That chain had many, many little coins hanging from it and was very valuable. My grandmother said we must save it until money was greatly needed. It was this chain with its coins that my mother planned to sell for my trip."

"Then everything is all right," said Nan in relief. "All you need do is sell the chain."

Fito shook his head. "No," he said soberly, "because now the chain is gone. My mother is very sad. And my father never speaks of it."

"But what happened to it?" asked Nick.

"It disappeared the day my mother and father took some friends to visit the ruins of Uxmal," said Fito. "They and their friends were in the ancient House of the Governor there. When they sat down for a little rest, one of the friends asked to see the chain. So my mother took it off and handed it to her. When the friend gave it back, my mother put the chain down on a ledge for a moment, while she removed a stone from her shoe. Meanwhile, the others went across the room and had their backs turned. When my mother went to pick up the chain, it was gone. They searched everywhere, but it was nowhere. Nor has anyone seen it since."

"But it must be somewhere," insisted Nick. "Haven't you ever gone back to look for it?"

"Sometimes my father has gone," Fito replied. "And sometimes he has taken me with him. But never will my mother go there. She says always that the place is haunted. I do not think that. But where could the chain have gone?"

Now Nick put an eager hand on Fito's shoulder. "Why don't we three go and hunt for it? Uncle Fred told us last night at supper that Uxmal is one of the places we are going to explore, while we are here."

Fito smiled slowly. "That would be very nice," he said. But Nick and Nan could see that he had little hope of ever finding the precious lost chain.

When they reached home, Fito needed no urging to stay for the fine big dinner that Senora Alvarez had cooked for them.

"The Senora is one of Merida's best cooks," he declared. And the Senora beamed as she put more crisp, hot tortillas on Fito's plate.

Happy days followed. Fito appeared every morning, and they went on an exploring trip. The twins never seemed to get tired, and they loved visiting Merida's fascinating markets. There must be presents for everyone, of course, and each of them had different ideas. Finally it was agreed that the handsome leather belts would please Father and Uncle Fred, and there were bright scarves for Mother and Senora Alvarez.

Not once did it occur to the twins that Fito might not be with them every day. But one morning he came as usual and said: "Tomorrow I must go with my father to the jungle, to help him and Rodolfo bring in the chicle."

"But you will be back day after tomorrow, won't you?" Nick asked.

Fito shook his head.

"It will be more days than one before I can come again," he told them.

That night when Uncle Fred returned home, he cried gaily up to the twins' balcony, "Come on down, you two. Big news!"

The twins came slowly down the stairs and across the patio.

"What's the matter?" asked Uncle Fred.

"Fito's going to the jungle tomorrow," the twins said together. "He won't be back for a long while."

Uncle Fred's eyes twinkled. "Don't you want to know about the big news?"

"Of course," they said. But their voices were not at all excited—only polite.

"Come to think of it, my news is going to include Fito, too," Uncle Fred said. The twins' faces brightened.

"This is my plan," their uncle continued. "We're going to Uxmal tomorrow, for a little exploring of those ruins. And I have the feeling that we're going to find Fito there. He and his father have gone in that direction for the chicle. Yes, that's exactly what is going to happen. We'll catch up with Fito and surprise him!"

This was different! The twins were as excited as Uncle Fred had expected them to be.

"And we can hunt for the chain together," said Nick.

That reminded Nan of something else. "Are the ruins at Uxmal really haunted, Uncle Fred?" she asked anxiously.

"Of course not," he laughed. But Nan wasn't so sure.

The sun was shining brightly when they started for Uxmal the next morning. They sped past the plaza and out from the city.

"An early start is good because now it is cool," Uncle Fred said. "It's not such a very long trip to Uxmal, and we can get in plenty of exploring before noon. It can be very hot and dusty there. The trees are low and give little shade."

"What is that strange plant all over everywhere?" asked Nick, waving at fields that seemed to stretch endlessly on and on.

"And why are those workmen cutting off the leaves?" asked Nan.

"Because that is one of the most useful plants in the world," Uncle Fred said. "It is henequen and those leaves have a fiber for making twine. Binder twine, it's called, and it's also known as sisal hemp. Making binder twine is Yucatan's famous industry. You will see many more henequen plantations before we get back."

Every now and then they passed an Indian's home, with its roof thatched high with grass, and its walls shaped in an oval with an opening in the center, but no windows. Sometimes a Mayan mother, carrying a little brown baby, would step out to wave at the passing car. They all had broad smiles like Fito's, and their teeth were shining white like his.

At last, in the distance across the flat country, a group of pyramids loomed against the sky. Nick and Nan knew they were coming to Uxmal, for in the book at home they had seen pictures of these very pyramids. When they reached the tallest one, Uncle Fred stopped the car and they all got out.

The pyramid towered high above them, with piles of loose stones at its base, and more stones placed here and there up its sides, in a kind of stairway.

"Look!" Nick cried excitedly. "There's still part of a house up at the top!"

"And see all the carving on the stones!" Nan exclaimed.

"Many people think that the decorations on this pyramid are the most beautiful of any on all the Mayan ruins," said Uncle Fred. "This pyramid is called the Pyramid of the Magician, or the Magician's House."

He waved at a pile of stones. "Those stones," he went on, "and those put back in place up the side, are part of the work that is going on to rebuild this pyramid so that it will look as it did when it was first erected, long ago."

Just then someone called loudly to Uncle Fred. Turning around, they saw a man standing in front of a thatched-roof house not far away.

"Why, there's my friend Rodolfo," said Uncle Fred. "I wonder why he's not out in the jungle? I'd better go over and see what he wants. He'll know where Fito is, too. Meanwhile, why don't you two take a stroll around the Magician's House? You can't get lost, and I'll be right back, anyway."

Nick and Nan were sure they had never been in so fascinating a place. After they had encircled the Pyramid of the Magician, they ran first in one direction, then in another, calling excitedly about each new discovery. Then they went more slowly, taking time to examine the carvings. They did not notice how much time had passed, and that Uncle Fred had not returned.

"How do you suppose they put these stones together?" Nick asked, after a while. "And what do you suppose they did the carving with? Father said they didn't have tools like ours."

"And look at these carvings of houses," said Nan. "They are just like the thatched Indian houses we've been seeing along the road today."

"Another thing I'd like to know," said Nick, "is why they had a stairway up the Pyramid of the Magician. Did someone live there at the top in that—"

"Nick!" interrupted Nan, and her voice was worried. "Where is Uncle Fred? We'd better go and look for him this minute."

When they ran around the Pyramid of the Magician to the spot where Uncle Fred had left them, they gasped. The car was gone! And no one was in sight over by the thatched-roof house.

"Goodness," said Nan.

"Yoo-hoo, Uncle Fred. Yoo-hooo!" called Nick. But there was no answer.

"Oh, dear," wailed Nan, very close to tears. "What shall we do?"

Nick was a little frightened, too. But he said quickly: "Now don't start worrying, Nan. Probably Uncle Fred is around on the other side of the Pyramid of the Magician, looking for us."

"In his car?" sniffed Nan.

"We-l-l," Nick hesitated. Then he added: "Anyway, we might as well hunt for him. That's better than standing here, looking at nothing."

Nan agreed, and they started off, calling, "Uncle Fred! Uncle Fred!" But there was still no answer, nor any sight of him or the car. There was a little rustle in the bushes near by, and Nan jumped in fright. Only a small iguana scampered out, trying to look like a much larger lizard than he was. Even the tiny hummingbird, green and glowing, which hesitated in front of them, did not arouse Nan's interest.

"He shines like an emerald," Nick said, but Nan did not answer. There was no one there among the ruins but themselves, and Nick was now as worried as Nan.

"I think we'd better stop going around and stay in one spot until someone comes," he said at last, as they climbed up onto one of the large mounds.

Sitting down on a stone, they looked at the ruins of the long low building in front of them. "This is a good place to wait," Nick went on, "because we can see all the other ruins from here, and the road to Merida, too."

"Will we have to be here all night?" wailed Nan.

"Of course not," Nick replied, more confidently than he felt. "Uncle Fred will be back any minute now."

There was nothing more to say then, and soon Nan began to cry quietly. Suddenly she whispered, "Listen! I'm sure I heard someone calling your name, Nick, from inside that low building over there. Oh-h-h," and a loud sob mingled with her tears, "I just knew this place was haunted!"

Nick stood up, listening intently. The voice was louder now, and there was no doubt that it was calling, "Nick!"

"That's no ghost, Nan!" Nick exclaimed. "That's a real voice. I'm going over there and take a look."

"You needn't think I'm going to stay here alone," cried Nan, jumping up.

As they came closer to the low building, they heard the voice again. Then who should appear in the entrance but Fito!

"Oh, there you are," he said. For a moment the twins were speechless.

"How did you get here?" Nick cried.

"Have you seen Uncle Fred?" Nan asked.

"Your uncle told me to find you," Fito replied, "and tell you that he will be back from the doctor's very soon."

"The doctor's!" gasped Nan.

"Is Uncle Fred hurt?" asked Nick.

Fito shook his head. "No, not your Uncle Fred. It's the government caretaker of the ruins, who lives over there. When my father and I, with Rodolfo, arrived here this morning we found that he had broken his leg. It was good that your uncle came here today in his car, so that the poor man could be taken to the next town to the doctor. That is where your Uncle Fred is now. My father and Rodolfo went along to help carry the injured man. I stayed behind to bring your uncle's message to you. But where have you been? I have searched long."

"We've been all over the ruins, I guess," Nick told him. "And everything was so interesting, we forgot all about Uncle Fred. When we did remember, the car was gone and so was everyone. Then when Nan heard your voice coming out of this building, she was sure your mother was right about Uxmal's being haunted."

Fito laughed. "I went in here because I thought you might be looking for my mother's chain. This is the Governor's House, you see."

The chain! They had forgotten all about their plan of searching for it. Now Nan said, "Why don't we look for it, while we're waiting for Uncle Fred?"

Fito shook his head. "I think it best to stay outside and wait. From that mound over there we can see the road. Then when the car comes, we can wave to your Uncle Fred at once, so that he will know you are safe," he said with a teasing little smile.

"All right," said Nan, ignoring the smile. "You can be telling us about the ruins. Then when Uncle Fred gets back, he can help us look for the chain."

Seated once more on the big stone, Nick and Nan looked about and waited for Fito to begin. In front of them, directly below, was the ancient ball court, Fito told them. Long ago the Mayans played a game rather like our basket ball, and it was very popular. Into the wall was built a stone ring, but up and down, not sideways like our basket ball basket today. Each team struggled to get the small ball through the ring.

"The great building with the inner court, over beyond," Fito continued, "was called the Nunnery. People are not sure that it was a Nunnery, but they think it was one, because there is only one entrance, you see. And no windows open on the outside at all."

"What is that strange building with a lot of openings?" asked Nick.

"That is called the House of Doves," replied Fito, "because those openings make it look like a dovecote."

He pointed to a small hill near it. "See where so many trees are growing," he said. "That is really another pyramid that hasn't been uncovered yet."

"I wish I could be here when they dig it up!" exclaimed Nan. "It would be like finding buried treasure, wouldn't it?"

"That is what it really is—buried treasure," agreed Fito. "It is interesting, too, to watch the men when they are at work rebuilding the Pyramid of the Magician. Some day it will again look just as it did in the long-ago time."

"Uncle Fred told us about that," said Nick. "But why do they call it the Magician's House, too, Fito?"

"There is a very old legend," Fito said, "that the Indians used to tell. Many years ago an old woman found a baby in the forest, who really was a dwarf. The old woman claimed he would be king. The ruler of Uxmal wanted to be rid of a rival, so he challenged the dwarf to a feat of strength. He declared that whoever succeeded in breaking a cocoanut on the head of the other should be the ruler. The dwarf agreed, because he was protected by the old woman's magic. His head was unharmed, but the ruler's was smashed by the blows, and the dwarf became king of all Uxmal, and lived on the pyramid which now bears his name."

"What a strange story," said Nick. "Is the Pyramid of the Magician, then, the palace that was built by the old woman's magic?"

"Well," laughed Fito, "that is what is said. Anyway, it has always been called that, as well as the House of the Magician."

"Listen!" exclaimed Nan suddenly. "I'm hearing strange noises again inside the Governor's House."

"Not so very strange," said Fito. "And not ghosts, either. What you hear are birds. Many swallows fly in and out of those ruins."

"Swallows!" cried Nan. "You mean swallows like those in Grandma's barn in Illinois?" Forgetting about being afraid, she ran to the Governor's House.

In a moment, the boys heard her calling from inside the ruins, "Come quickly!" When they rushed inside, they found Nan looking anxiously at a small nest on the wall.

"As I came in," she cried, "hundreds of swallows flew out. And I'm sure I saw one leave that nest. Probably nobody has been in here since the nest was built. And now the mother will be too frightened to come back and the baby birds will die."

"I don't think so," said Fito. "When we leave, the birds will return. Besides, the eggs in the nest may not have hatched."

"I'm going to find out," declared Nan, running to the wall.

She started to climb up on the jagged stones. Nick ran over to the wall and held tightly to the hem of her dress.

"Come back, Nan," he said. "If you must know about it, I'll do the climbing. I'm better at it than you are."

So Nan slid down, and slowly and carefully Nick climbed the wall to the nest.

"Everything's all right, Nan," he called. "Just eggs here—one, two, th—!"

Then for no reason that Fito and Nan could understand he shouted, "For goodness sake! Oh, my goodness! Look! Look!"

From where they stood Nan and Fito could see nothing, but Nick was scrambling down the wall in double-quick time.

"Look!" he repeated breathlessly, when he stood once more beside his sister and Fito. "Look!"

Then he opened his hand and there, bright and shining, was a little chain with dangling golden coins!

"It's Fito's!" gasped Nan. "It's the lost chain. Oh, Fito, isn't it just too wonderful?"

But Fito could not speak. He could only stare at the long lost chain, and touch it wonderingly with his finger.

"But where was it, Nick?" Nan wanted to know.

"Woven into the nest," Nick told them. "Now you can come to the United States for a visit, Fito."

"Here we are folks," said a familiar voice at the entrance. "The patient is doing nicely, I'm happy to report. But what's all the excitement about?"

It was Uncle Fred, coming in with Fito's father, and Rodolfo. Fito was far from speechless then. Excitedly, he, too, joined in the story of the chain.

"And you will let Fito come and visit us now, won't you?" Nan asked Fito's father, when they had told all about everything.

"Yes, Mees Nan, yes, yes," he promised, with a smile as broad as his son's.

Talking gaily, they all went out to Uncle Fred's car, and climbed in. Tomorrow, they agreed, would be plenty of time for Fito's father and Fito and Rodolfo to start after chicle once more. Today the glad news of the chain must be taken to Fito's mother and all the neighbors.

"Good-by, Uxmal, and thank you," cried Nan.

As the car started off she waved to the Pyramid of the Magician.

"Never, never will I forget this wonderful day," said Nick.

"I, too, shall always remember the—shall I say haunted?—Governor's House, Nan," Fito smiled.

Nan's happy smile answered Fito's. "All right," she said.